Dear Parent:

Congratulations! Your child is taking the first steps on an exciting journey. The destination? Independent reading!

STEP INTO READING® will help your child get there. The program offers five steps to reading success. Each step includes fun stories and colorful art. There are also Step into Reading Sticker Books, Step into Reading Math Readers, Step into Reading Write-In Readers, Step into Reading Phonics Readers, and Step into Reading Phonics First Steps! Boxed Sets—a complete literacy program with something for every child.

Learning to Read, Step by Step!

Ready to Read   Preschool–Kindergarten
• big type and easy words • rhyme and rhythm • picture clues
For children who know the alphabet and are eager to begin reading.

Reading with Help   Preschool–Grade 1
• basic vocabulary • short sentences • simple stories
For children who recognize familiar words and sound out new words with help.

Reading on Your Own   Grades 1–3
• engaging characters • easy-to-follow plots • popular topics
For children who are ready to read on their own.

Reading Paragraphs   Grades 2–3
• challenging vocabulary • short paragraphs • exciting stories
For newly independent readers who read simple sentences with confidence.

Ready for Chapters   Grades 2–4
• chapters • longer paragraphs • full-color art
For children who want to take the plunge into chapter books but still like colorful pictures.

STEP INTO READING® is designed to give every child a successful reading experience. The grade levels are only guides. Children can progress through the steps at their own speed, developing confidence in their reading, no matter what their grade.

Remember, a lifetime love of reading starts with a single step!

For sweet Ramona

Library of Congress Cataloging-in-Publication Data
Jordan, Apple.
The sweetest spring / by Apple Jordan;
illustrated by Francesco Legramandi & Gabriella Matta. — 1st ed.
    p. cm. — (Step into reading. Step 2)
Summary: Six Disney princesses enjoy springtime activities in separate, easy-to-read vignettes.
ISBN: 978-0-375-84810-0 (trade)
ISBN: 978-0-375-94810-7 (lib. bdg.)
[1. Spring—Fiction. 2. Princesses—Fiction. 3. Stories in rhyme.] I. Legramandi, Francesco, ill.
II. Matta, Gabriella, ill. III. Title.
PZ8.3.J7645Sw 2008
[E]—dc22
2007018145

Printed in the United States of America   10 9 8 7 6 5 4 3 2 1   First Edition

STEP INTO READING®

STEP 2

Disney

♦ PRINCESS

The
Sweetest Spring

By Apple Jordan

Illustrated by

Francesco Legramandi & Gabriella Matta

Random House 🏠 New York

Spring is here!

There is much to do.

Sweep the floors
and mop up, too.

Clean the windows.

Scrub the floor.

Dust the tables.

Wash the door.

Singing makes
the chores more fun.
One, two, three!
The work is done.

The house is ready
to welcome spring.
Sharing the chores
is the sweetest thing.

Winter is over.
Now it is spring.
Ariel and her sisters
sing for the king.

Everyone gathers
to see all the flowers.

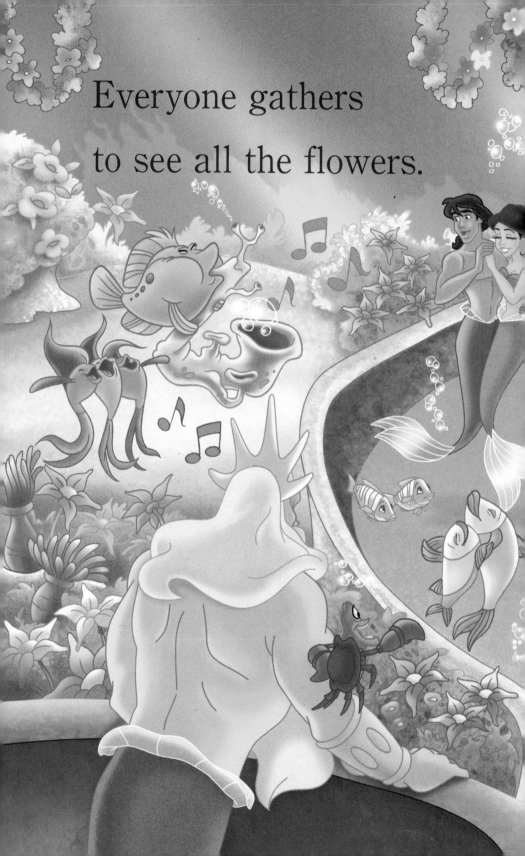

They dance and sing
for hours and hours.

The salt water is warm.
It smells of spring.
A springtime fair
is the sweetest thing.

Spring is here!
Jasmine has one wish—
to see a spring shower.
<u>Splish-splash-splish!</u>

Rain showers are
a sure sign
it is spring.

Splashing in puddles
is the sweetest thing.

Spring is here!
Wake up, friends!

The winter slumber
has come to an end.

A robin comes out
to sing a spring song.
The bumblebees are
buzzing right along.

The animals are happy.

At last it is spring.

Greeting our friends

is the sweetest thing.

Cinderella and her prince
share a spring stroll.
They see a rabbit
peeking out of its hole.

Flowers bud.

Roses bloom.

Wedding bells ring

for this new

bride and groom.

The happy couple shares
the wonders of spring.

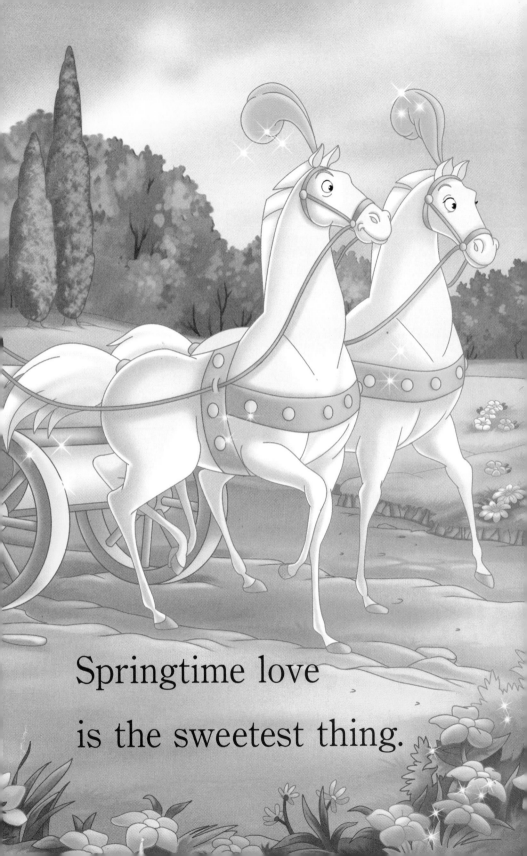

Springtime love
is the sweetest thing.

Belle makes a garden.
There is much to do.

She wants plants
and pretty flowers, too.

She plants some seeds,
all in a row.

The soil

needs water.

It helps

flowers grow.

Belle waits . . .

and waits . . .

for days and hours.

The garden has grown

many pretty flowers.

The yard is filled with
the flowers of spring.
Planting a garden
is the sweetest thing!